CC CLAUS

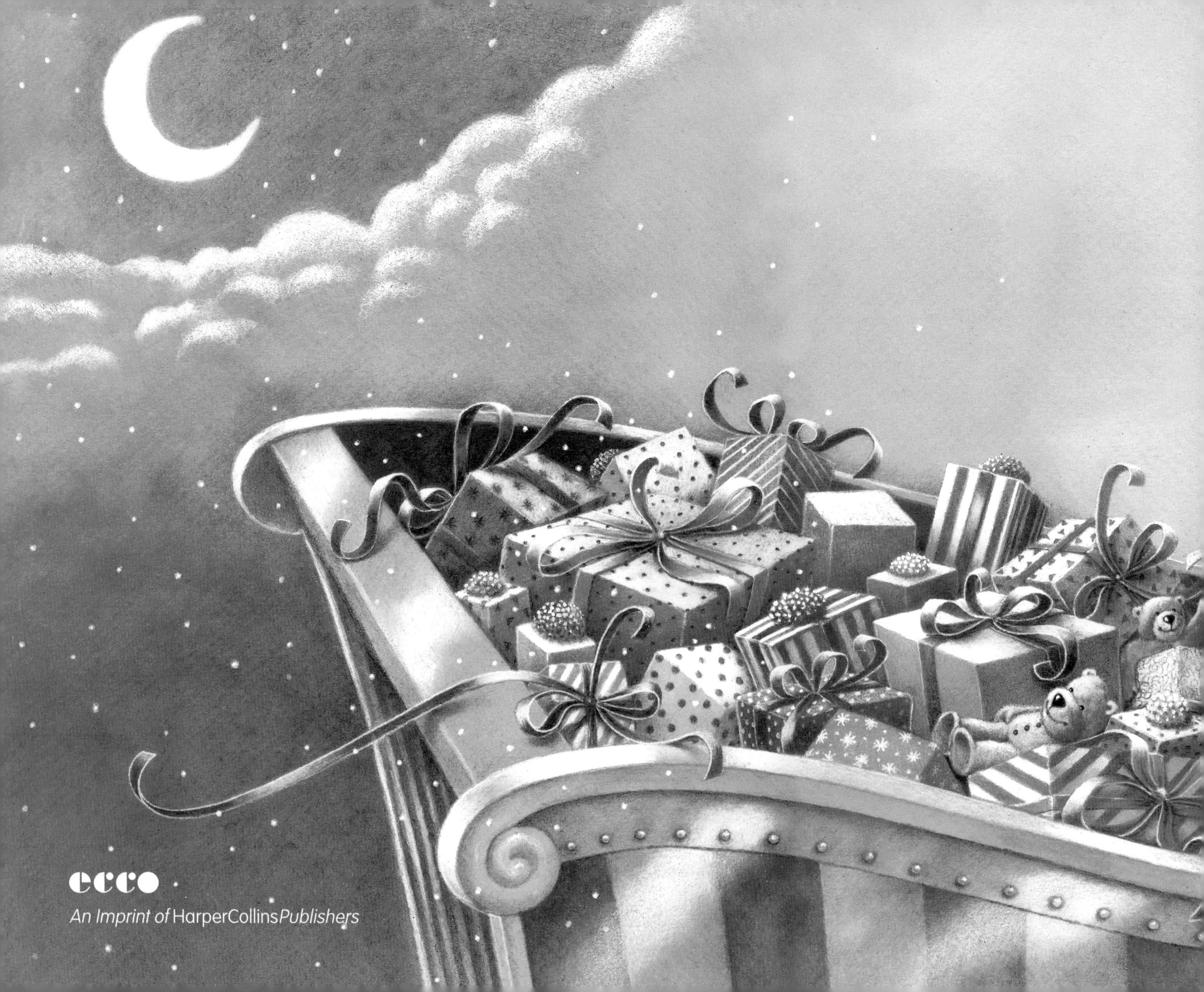

ecco
An Imprint of HarperCollins*Publishers*

CC CLAUS

A BASEBALL CHRISTMAS STORY

CC SABATHIA

WRITTEN WITH **RAY NEGRON** AND ILLUSTRATIONS BY **LAURA SEELEY**

I'd like to thank a couple of people who helped me by posing for the book:
Debbi Hancock McIntyre, Karen Danner-Reed, Dana Yarger
—LAURA SEELEY

HarperCollins books may be purchased for educational, business, or sales promotional use. For information please e-mail the Special Markets Department at SPsales@harpercollins.com.

FIRST EDITION

Designed by Suet Yee Chong

Library of Congress Cataloging-in-Publication Data has been applied for.

ISBN 978-0-06-231841-1

14 15 16 17 18   PC   10 9 8 7 6 5 4 3 2 1

WORDS CAN'T SAY HOW MUCH I LOVE MY FAMILY:
MY WIFE, AMBER; AND MY KIDS, CARSTEN, JAEDEN, CYIA, AND CARTER;
MY MOM, MARGIE, AND MY GRANDMOTHER ETHEL RUFUS.

WE HAVE ALWAYS BEEN IN THIS JOURNEY TOGETHER.
—CC SABATHIA

TO POLICE OFFICER JON-ERIK NEGRON AND ALL THE POLICE OFFICERS
AND FIREFIGHTERS THROUGHOUT THIS GREAT COUNTRY.

THANK YOU SILVER SHIELD FOR ALL YOU DO.

THANK YOU ALSO TO TONY GWYNN,
A TRUE GENTLEMAN WHO WOULD HAVE HELPED THE BOSS AND SANTA.
—RAY NEGRON

It was Christmas Eve, and everything was ready at the Sabathia house. The stockings were hung. The cards had been mailed. The only things missing were the presents that Santa would leave under the tree.

Jaeden, Cyia, and Carter had already gone to bed. Only Carsten was still awake, sitting by the sofa where CC was reading his fan mail.

A tiny envelope fell out of the pile. "Daddy!" Carsten said. "This one is addressed to Santa Claus."

Carsten gathered all his baseball cards and hopped up to see. The envelope had not been sealed, and the letter fell out.

CC shook his head. "It's a shame Santa won't get this letter in time."

"Why not?" Carsten asked.

Dear Santa, We had a terrible flood and lost all our toys. I don't mind, but my brothers Homer and Daniel miss their baseballs and gloves. Can you bring them new ones? Love, Anabel

"It's too late for the mail to get it to the North Pole."

"Oh, Daddy! Can't we take it there ourselves?" Carsten asked. "We have to help Anabel and her brothers! Pleeeeeeease?"

CC thought for a moment. "Okay. Get dressed very warmly. We're going to the North Pole!"

Carsten tucked the letter into his pocket with his baseball cards, and they piled into the car. "How do we get there, Daddy?" Carsten asked excitedly.

"Easy," CC answered. "We go north!"

They drove on big highways, small roads, and dirt tracks. The dirt tracks changed to snowy lanes. It seemed like forever to Carsten, but at last they could see the Elves' Toyshop.

Carsten and CC got out of the car and hurried to find Santa.

"Here's a letter that came to me by mistake!" called out CC. "Somewhere there are two little boys who need balls and gloves to play baseball!"

Santa pulled the letter from the tiny envelope.

As he read, he sighed.

"I don't know, CC," he answered. "There have been many storms this year, and hundreds of kids lost their toys. I might not be able to finish everything. And I'm feeling under the weather too. There's just not enough time. I need help!"

"I know just the person," CC said, taking out his special cell phone and dialing 0. "Hello, Boss?" Quickly he explained the problem.

"I'll be right there," said a voice.

And a minute later Mr. Steinbrenner walked through the door.

"Let's get to work!" he ordered. "Christmas is almost here!"

"But there are only three of us." CC was worried. "I wish we had some more people to help."

Carsten pulled all of his baseball cards out of his pocket. "They'd help, if they could," he said, looking at the faces of his baseball heroes. "I wish we could call them."

"Who says we can't?" barked Mr. Steinbrenner.

"CC, use your special phone. Get me Mantle. Get me DiMaggio and Ted Williams. Get me Ruth and Gehrig. Get me Maris and Munson and Murcer and Martin. Get me Catfish, Elston Howard, Hank Greenberg, and Satchel Paige.

"Don't forget Rizzuto. And Jackie Mitchell too.

"You used to play in Cleveland, so get me Bob Feller. Also Roberto Clemente, Jackie Robinson, Willie Stargell, Paul Blair, and Tetsuharu Kawakami. Get me all of them and have them report here right away.

"And make sure you get me Ray the Batboy!"

One by one, CC went through the numbers on his phone until he reached everybody. Soon they had all arrived.

"Okay, guys, we have a lot of work to do," Mr. Steinbrenner called out. "Blair and Kawakami, you make bats. DiMaggio and Maris, you do gloves. Elston and Mitchell, do baseballs. Munson, you have train sets. Catfish and Murcer, you have dolls."

"Dolls!" Catfish said.

"Dolls. And don't forget to make a real nice one for Anabel!"

Everyone got to work. As soon as Jackie Mitchell finished a baseball, she'd toss it to Babe Ruth, who'd pop it in a box. Bobby Murcer sat in his rocking chair painting faces on dolls.

Mickey Mantle made board games. Phil Rizzuto did action figures. Satchel Paige made teddy bears, and Billy Martin finished all the cowboy boots.

The elves taught Lou Gehrig and Ted Williams how to make video games. Willie Stargell wired wheels on the toy trucks, and Ray the Batboy painted all the scenes in the picture books.

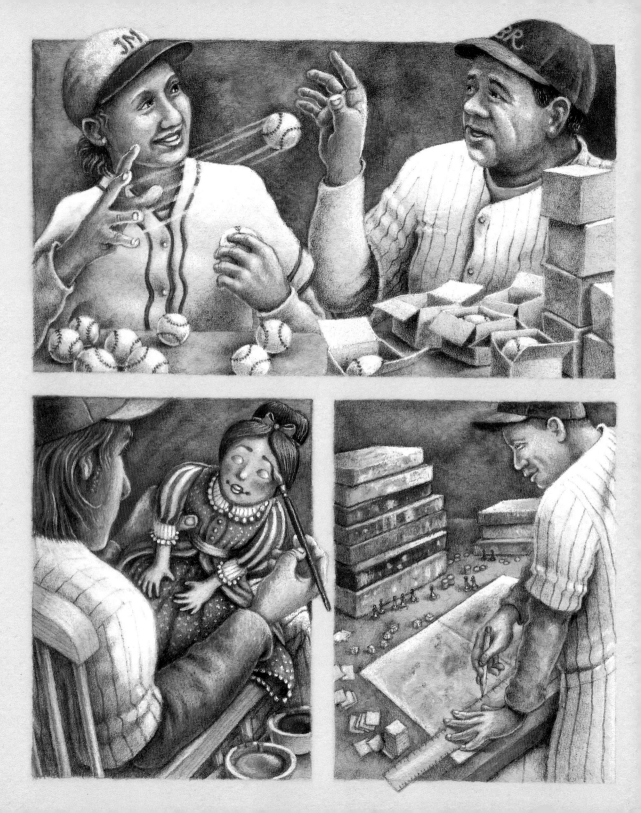

Roberto Clemente packed boxes with warm coats and thick, soft blankets. Jackie Robinson and Hank Greenberg sorted fuzzy socks and cozy mittens.

The Boss was in charge of wrapping. CC and Carsten piled the presents onto the sleigh.

But Santa still wasn't smiling. In fact, he was coughing and sneezing. And his nose was redder than Rudolph's.

"Oh dear, I don't think I'll be able to make it this year," he moaned. "I don't know what to do. I don't want to disappoint all the children!"

"No problem!" said Mr. Steinbrenner. "CC, you can wear Santa's suit and go."

Carsten's eyes lit up. "Can we, Daddy? Please? Can we make sure that all the children get their presents? Especially Anabel and Homer and Daniel?"

"But I'll never fit into his suit," said CC. "I'm too tall!"

Babe spoke up. "Why don't you use mine? You need it more than I do these days anyway!"

"Okay. Let's do it!" CC said.

Babe Ruth's suit was a perfect fit. And when CC put on Santa's hat and mittens, everybody cheered.

"You're CC Claus!" Carsten cried proudly.

"And you can be his elf, Carsten," Mr. Steinbrenner said, "and read him the list!"

Finally the reindeer were ready and the sleigh was packed.

Santa showed CC how to work the reins and taught him the magic spell to get up and down the chimneys.

They were away!

"Merry Christmas!" Carsten yelled.

"Feliz Navidad!" Roberto Clemente called back.

It was a long night. They visited country homes, city homes, farm homes, mountain homes, beach homes, and houses of every shape, size, and color. Carsten lost count. He hadn't realized what a big job Santa had each year.

Just before the sun came up, they visited
the last house on the list.

They put all the presents under the tree, and then sent the reindeer and sleigh back to the North Pole.

CC and Carsten climbed into their beds and fell fast asleep.

Soon they heard Jaeden, Cyia, and Carter laughing and screaming.
"Daddy! Santa was here!"

"Was he?" CC said.

"Yes! And he left lots of presents!"

"Oh, did he?" CC answered, winking at Carsten,
who smiled back at him. . . .

PAUL BLAIR

(1944–2013)

CENTER FIELDER

Played for the Baltimore Orioles, New York Yankees, and the Cincinnati Reds

Paul Blair was a member of three world championship teams, including the Baltimore Orioles and the New York Yankees. He was one of the greatest center fielders of all time, winning eight gold gloves. He was known lovingly by his teammates as "Motormouth" because he was always talking.

ROBERTO CLEMENTE

(1934–1972)

RIGHT FIELDER

Played for the Pittsburgh Pirates

Clemente clobbered 3,000 hits in his career, batting .414 in the 1971 World Series. He died in a plane crash at 38 years old, flying relief supplies to earthquake victims.

JOSEPH PAUL "JOE" DIMAGGIO

(1914–1999)

CENTER FIELDER

Played for the New York Yankees

In 1941, DiMaggio got at least one hit in 56 games in a row, one of the most amazing feats in baseball. He was named the sport's greatest living player in 1969.

ROBERT WILLIAM ANDREW "BOB" FELLER

(1918–2010)

PITCHER

Played for the Cleveland Indians

Called "Rapid Robert" for his sizzling fastball, Feller struck out 2,581 players in his career.

HENRY LOUIS "LOU" GEHRIG

(1903–1941)

FIRST BASEMAN

Played for the New York Yankees

Nicknamed "The Iron Horse," Gehrig had 13 seasons in a row with over 100 runs scored and 100 RBI.

HENRY BENJAMIN "HANK" GREENBERG

(1911–1986)

FIRST BASEMAN

Played for the Detroit Tigers and the Pittsburgh Pirates

Greenberg hit 331 home runs in his career, and in 1938 he came close to beating Babe Ruth's record for home runs in a single year.

ELSTON GENE HOWARD

(1929–1980)

CATCHER, LEFT FIELDER, AND FIRST BASEMAN

Played for the Kansas City Monarchs, the New York Yankees, and the Boston Red Sox

As a catcher, Howard was known for how well he coached pitchers, using his knowledge of the hitters they would be facing.

JAMES AUGUSTUS "CATFISH" HUNTER

(1946–1999)

PITCHER

Played for the Kansas City A's, the Oakland A's, and the New York Yankees

Known for his precise, controlled pitching, Hunter pitched a perfect game in 1968 and was awarded the American League Cy Young Award in 1974.

TETSUHARU "THE GOD OF BATTING" KAWAKAMI

(1920–2013)

FIRST BASEMAN

Played for the Yomiuri Giants

The first player in Japanese pro baseball to achieve 2,000 hits, Kawakami went on to manage the Giants, who won 11 Japan Series championships under his leadership.

MICKEY CHARLES MANTLE

(1931–1995)

CENTER FIELDER

Played for the New York Yankees

Mantle hit 536 home runs in his career and had a .298 batting average. He won three Most Valuable Player Awards.

ROGER EUGENE MARIS

(1934–1985)

RIGHT FIELDER

Played for the New York Yankees, the St. Louis Cardinals, the Kansas City A's, and the Cleveland Indians

In 1961, Maris hit 61 home runs, breaking Babe Ruth's record for home runs in a single season.

ALFRED MANUEL "BILLY" MARTIN

(1928–1989)

SECOND BASEMAN, SHORTSTOP, AND THIRD BASEMAN

Played for the New York Yankees

After retiring as a player, Martin brilliantly managed five major league baseball teams.

VIRNE BEATRICE "JACKIE" MITCHELL

(1912–1987)

PITCHER

Played for the Chattanooga Lookouts

In 1931, Mitchell, just 17 years old, struck out both Babe Ruth and Lou Gehrig in a single exhibition game against the Yankees.

THURMAN LEE MUNSON

(1947–1979)

CATCHER

Played for the New York Yankees

Captain of the Yankees, Munson was a team leader who made 1,558 hits and 113 home runs in his career.

BOBBY RAY MURCER

(1946–2008)

OUTFIELDER

Played for the New York Yankees, the Chicago Cubs, and the San Francisco Giants

Murcer's first hit in the major leagues was a home run. He became a five-time All-Star.

LEROY ROBERT "SATCHEL" PAIGE

(1906–1982)

PITCHER

Played for the Kansas City Monarchs, the Cleveland Indians, the St. Louis Browns, and the Kansas City Athletics

Playing in the Negro Leagues, Paige was known for his creative and tricky pitching, baffling hitters with his "Bat Dodger" and "Hesitation Pitch."

PHILLIP FRANCIS "PHIL" RIZZUTO

(1917–2007)

SHORTSTOP

Played for the New York Yankees

Rizzuto helped the Yankees win the World Series seven times out of nine and was named the American League's Most Valuable Player in 1950.

JACK ROOSEVELT "JACKIE" ROBINSON

(1919–1972)

SECOND BASEMAN

Played for the Kansas City Monarchs and the Brooklyn Dodgers

The first African-American player in the major leagues, Robinson helped the Dodgers win the World Series in 1955 and was a six-time All-Star. He stole home 19 times in his career.

GEORGE HERMAN "BABE" RUTH

(1895–1948)

RIGHT FIELDER AND PITCHER

Played for the Boston Red Sox, the New York Yankees, and the Boston Braves

Called "the Sultan of Swat," Ruth hit 714 home runs in his career.

WILVER DORNELL "WILLIE" STARGELL

(1940–2001)

RIGHT FIELDER

Played for the Pittsburgh Pirates

A powerful left-handed hitter, Stargell clobbered 475 home runs in his career.

THEODORE SAMUEL "TED" WILLIAMS

(1918–2002)

LEFT FIELDER

Played for the Boston Red Sox

One of the greatest hitters in baseball, Williams hit 521 home runs in his career and was the last major league player with a batting average over .400 in a single season.